This book is
ultimately dedicated
to our baby girl
Amara Celestine J. Basa,
sons
Niel Michael J. Basa
and
Jasper Miguel J. Basa.

INTRODUCTION

Learning How To Write The Alphabet is an introduction to Alphabet by using images. Toddlers first recognize letters by its sound. Recognizing the images will help them identify, differentiate and pronounce the 26 English alphabets.

What made this book special is that all words used were animal names from A-Z with images as an example.

This book will also help kids write the alphabet for the first time by tracing down the letters.

TABLE OF CONTENTS

THE ENGLISH ALPHABETS

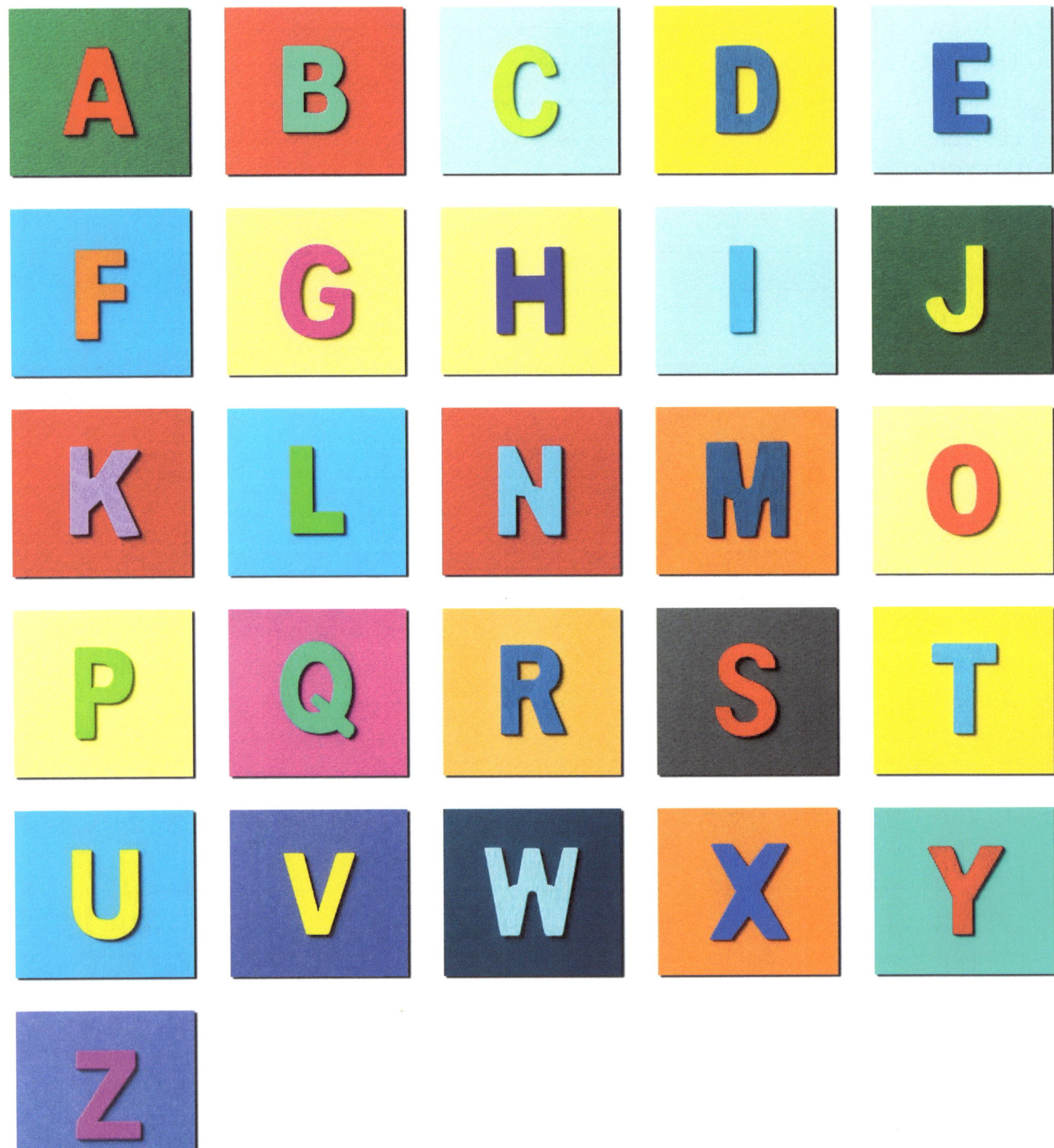

Aa

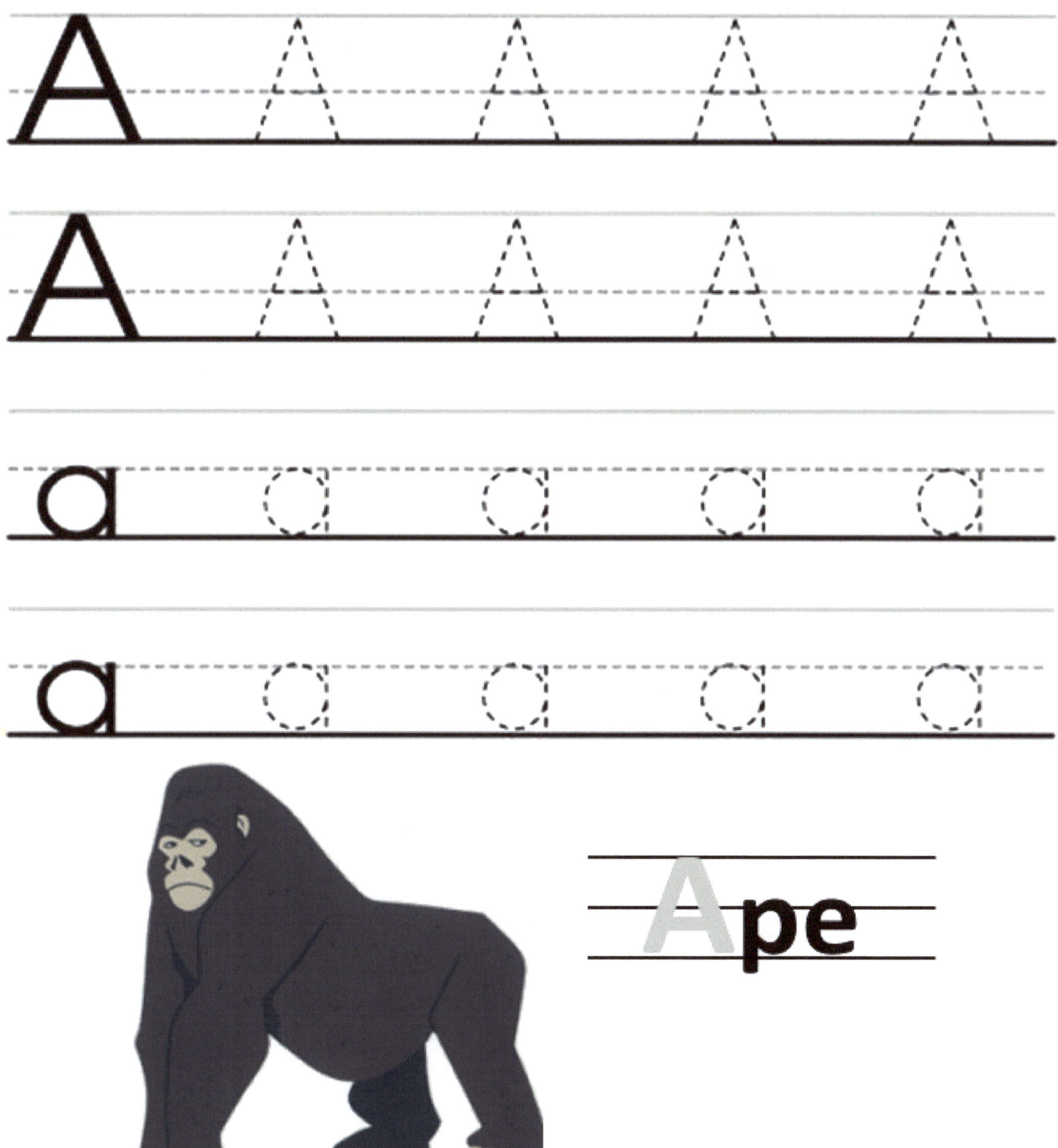

Addax

Ant

Anoa

Anole

Auk

Alpaca

Bb

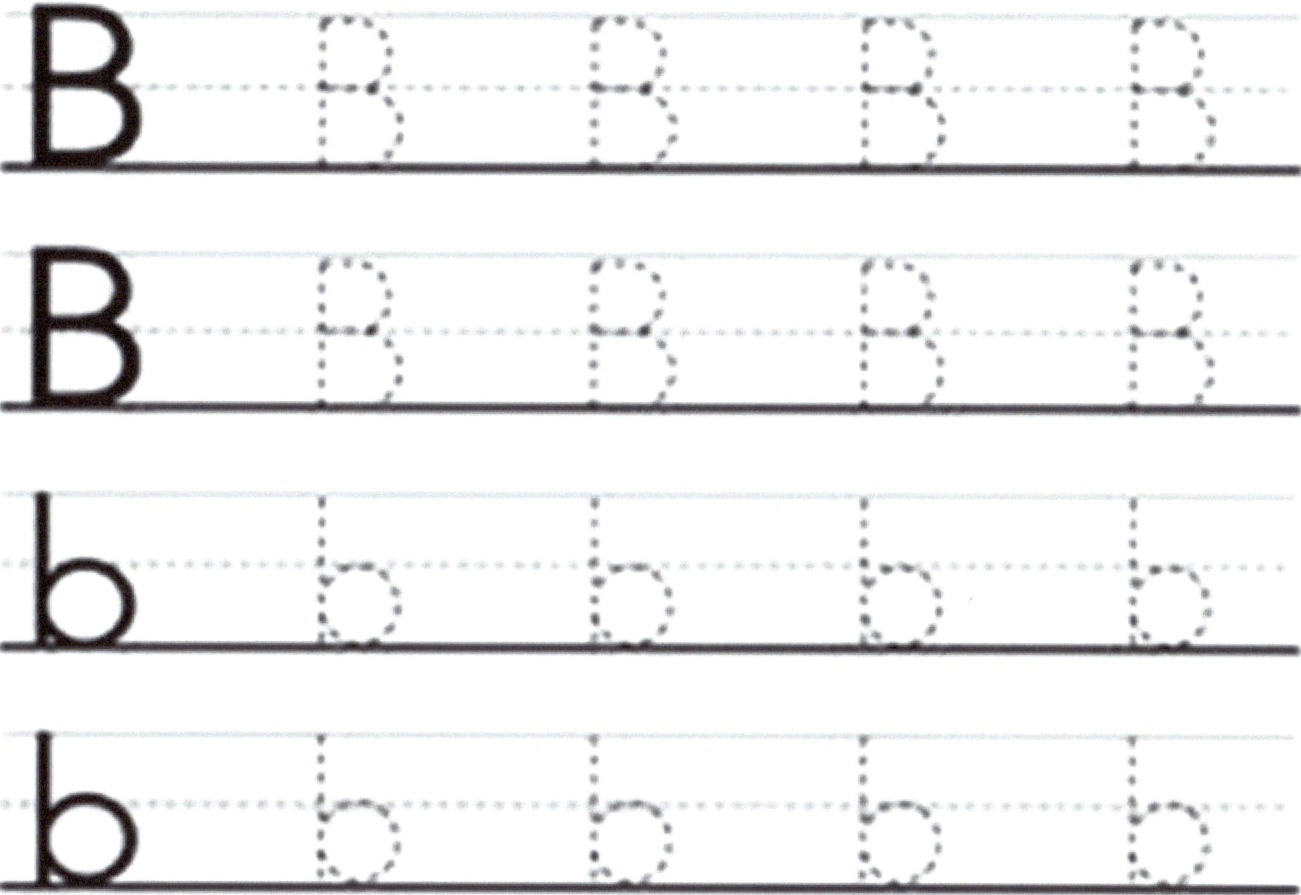

Baboon

Bat

Bug

Bear

Beaver

Bee

Bird

Cc

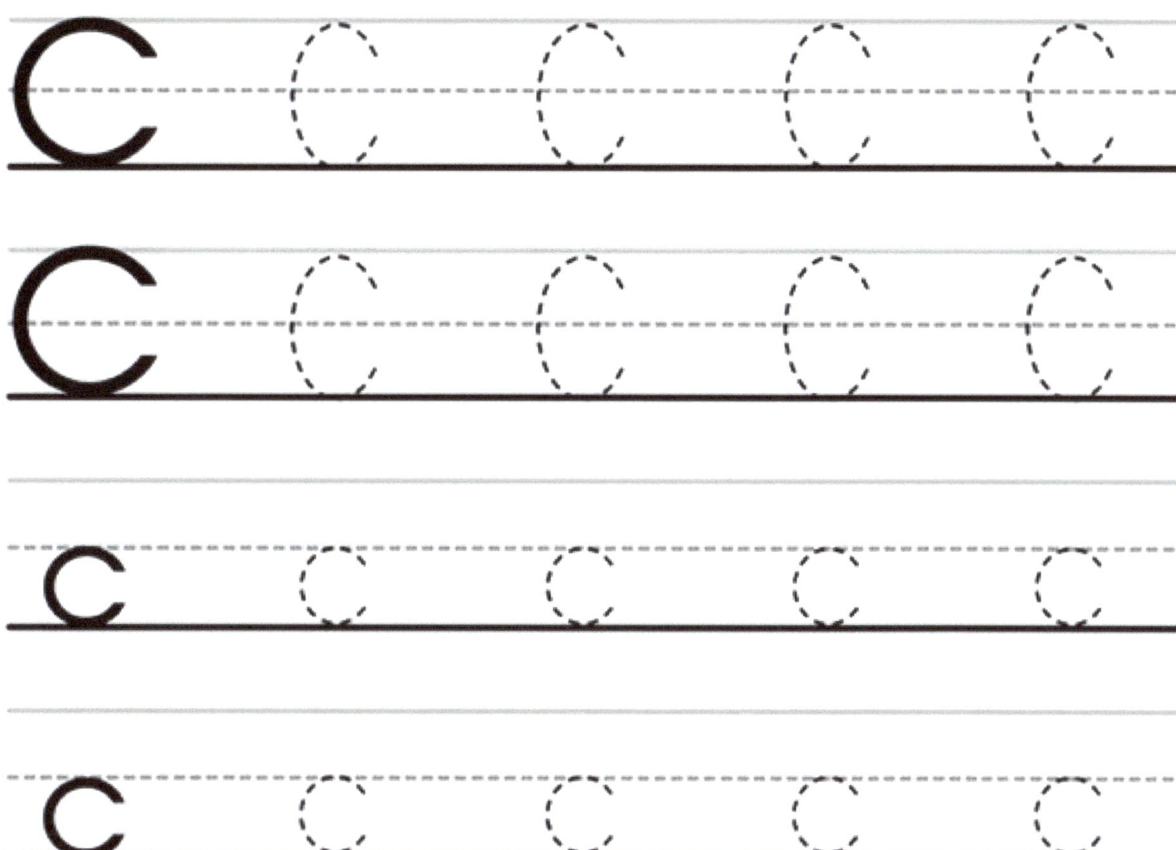

Chicken

Cat

Cheetah

Camel

Clam

Crow

Coyote

Dd

D
D
d
d

Deer

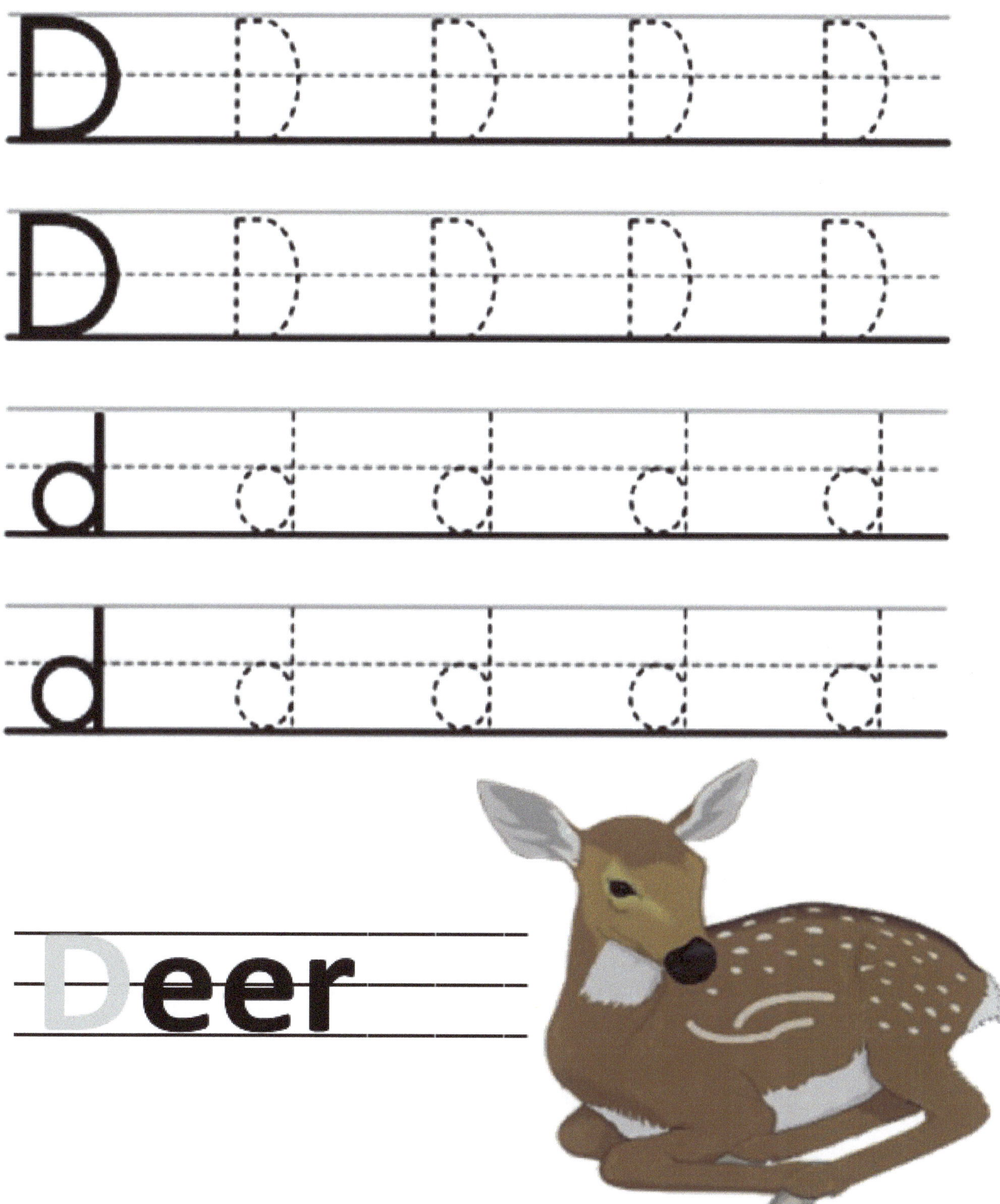

Dog

Dolphin

Donkey

Dove

Duck

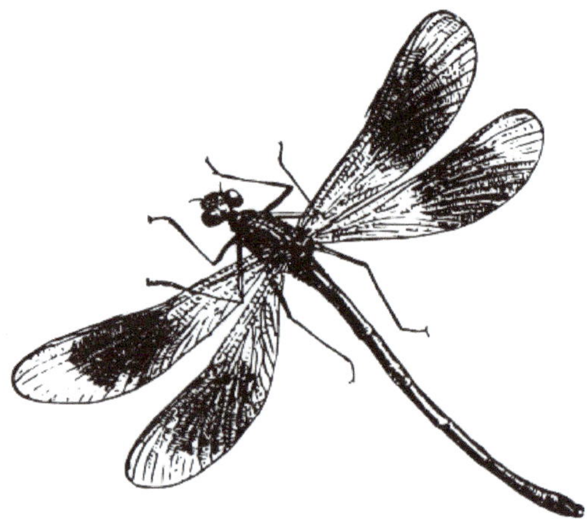

Dragonfly

Ee

Elephant

Eagle

Eel

Elk

Emu

Egret

Eider

Ff

F

F

f

f

Ferret

Falcon

Fox

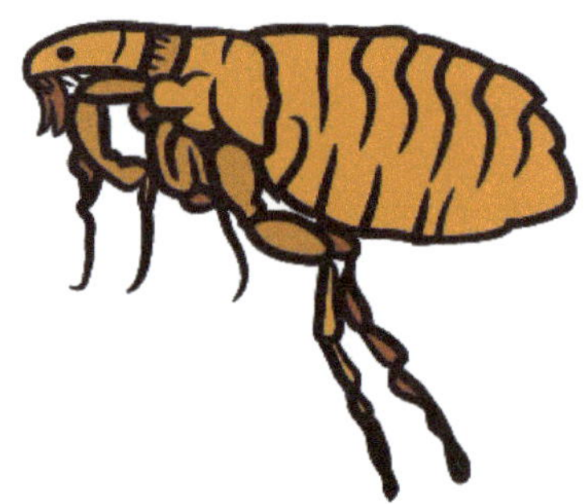

Flea

Fly

Fossa

Frog

Gg

G

G

g

g

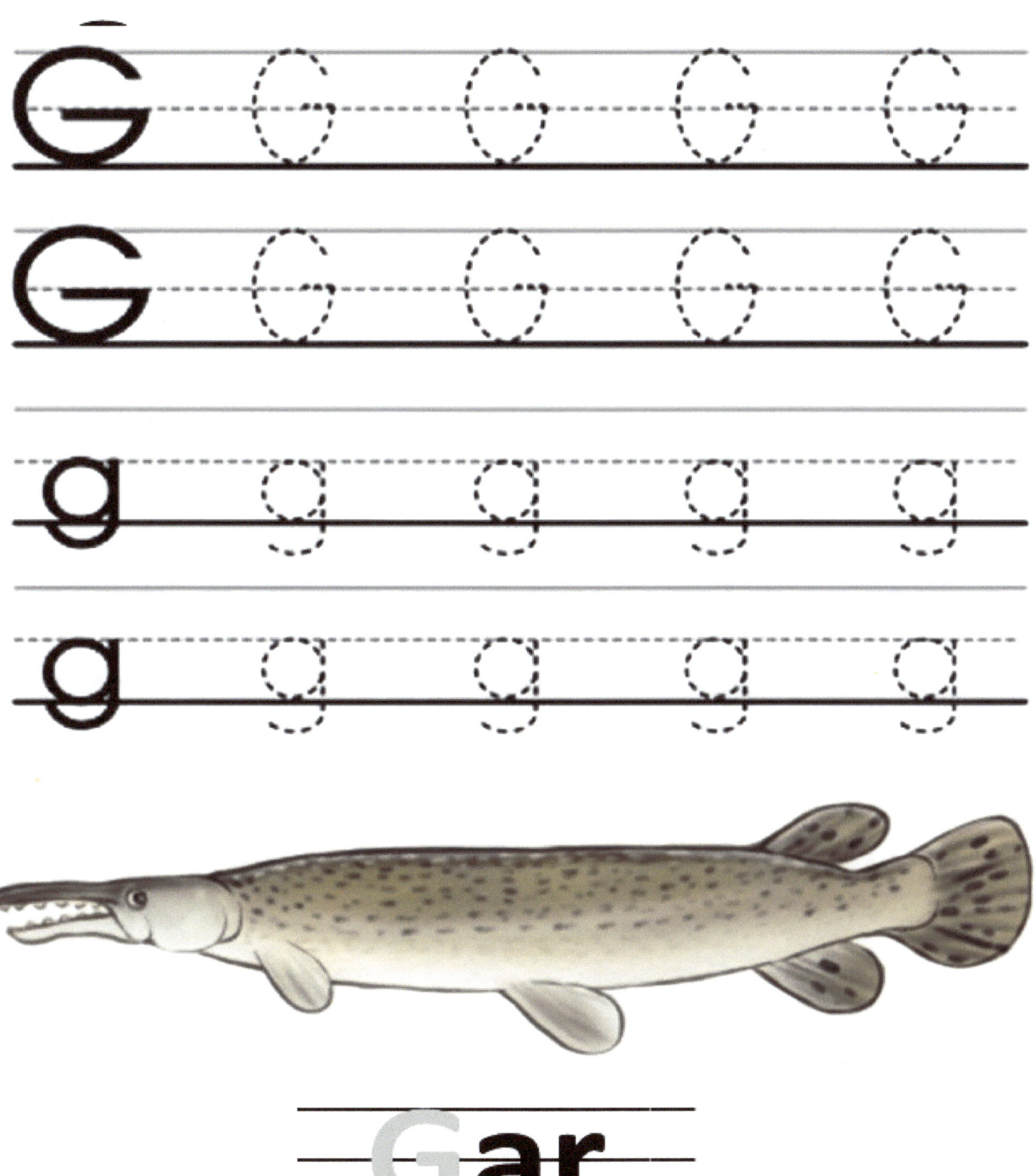

Gar

Goat

Gull

Giraffe

Goose

Gnu

Gorilla

Hh

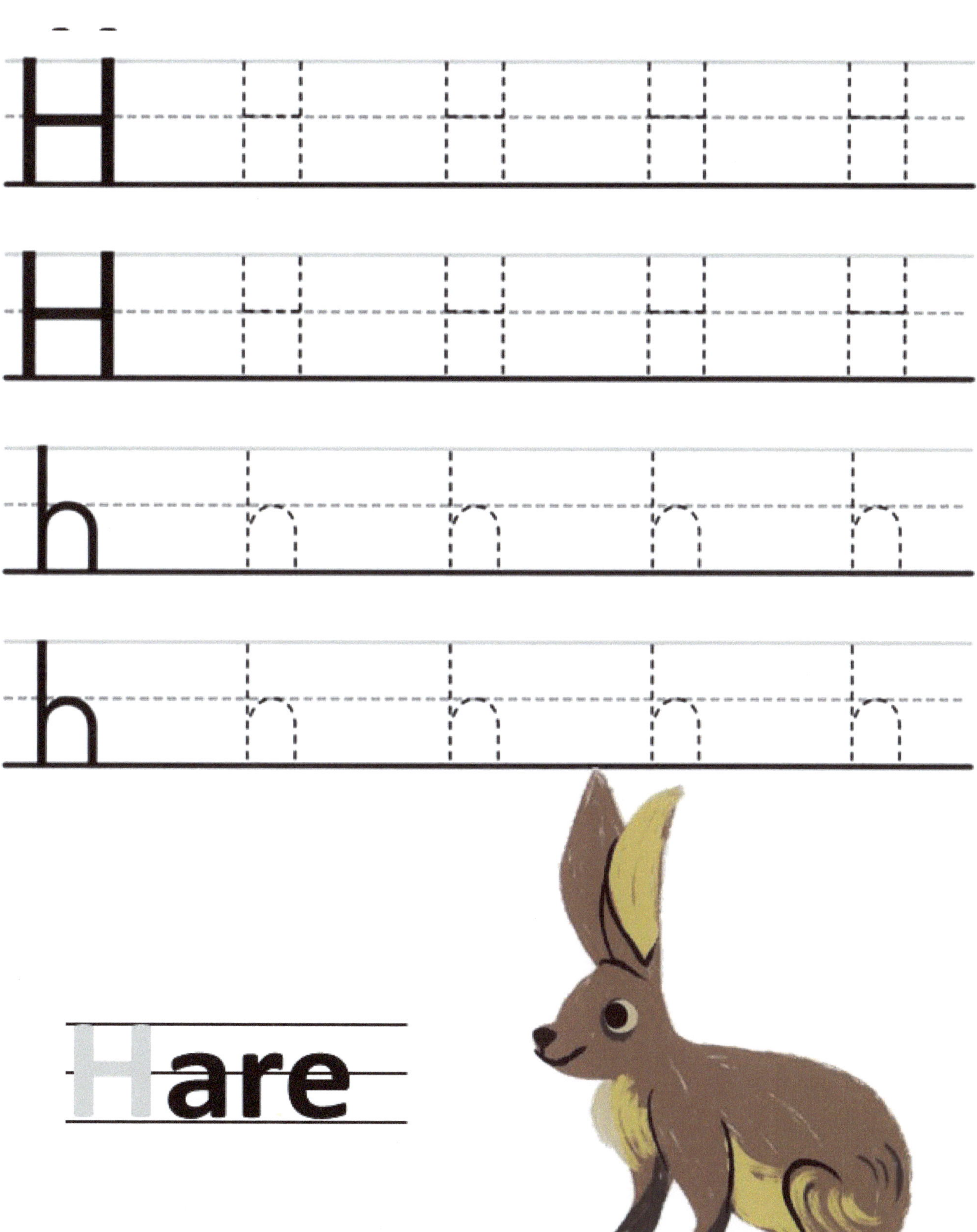

Hare

Hornet

Heron

Horse

Hamster

Hawk

Hyena

Ii

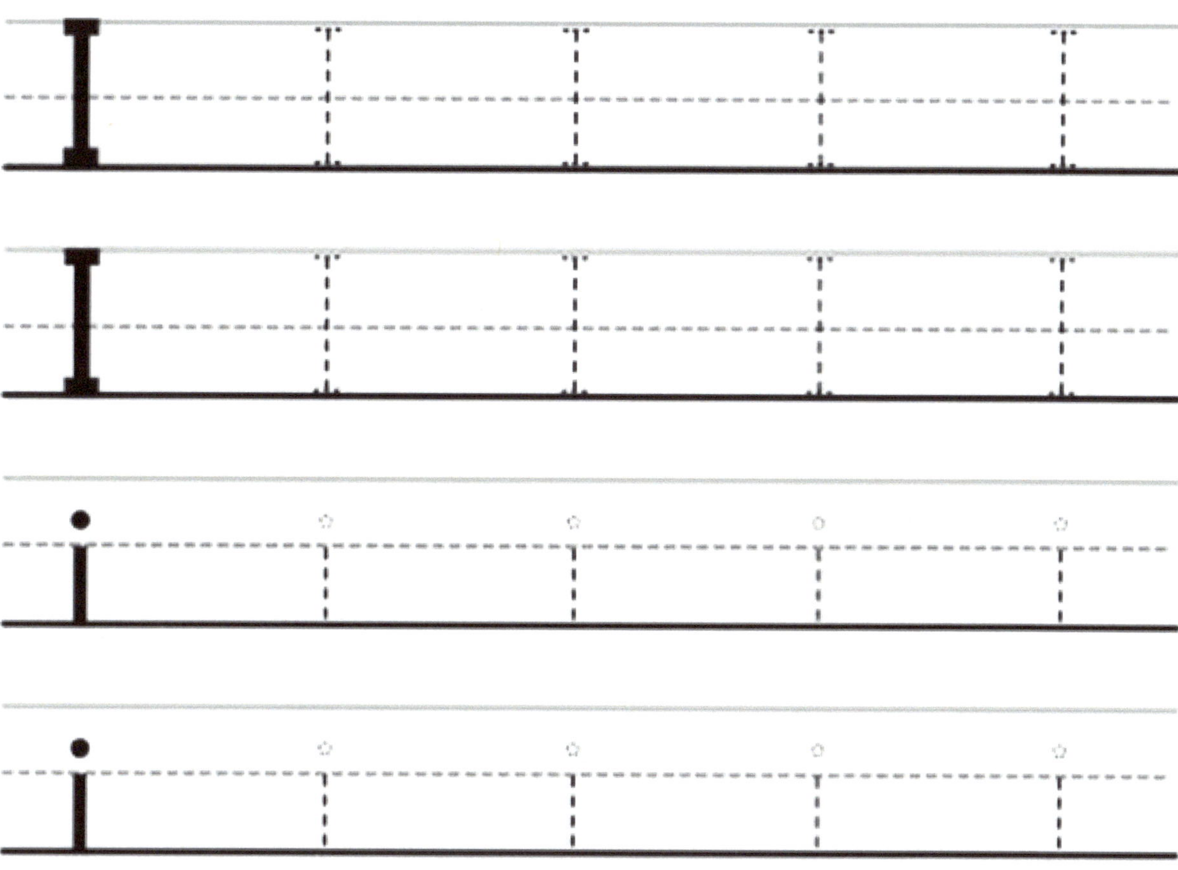

Insect

Ibex

Ibis

Icterid

Iguana

Impala

Indri

Jj

J J J J J

J J J J J

j j j j j

j j j j j

Jellyface

Jay

Jackal

Jaguar

Jacana

Jabiru

Jack russel

Kk

K k

Kakapo

Kiwi

Kitten

Kangaroo

Koi

Koala

Kestrel

Ll

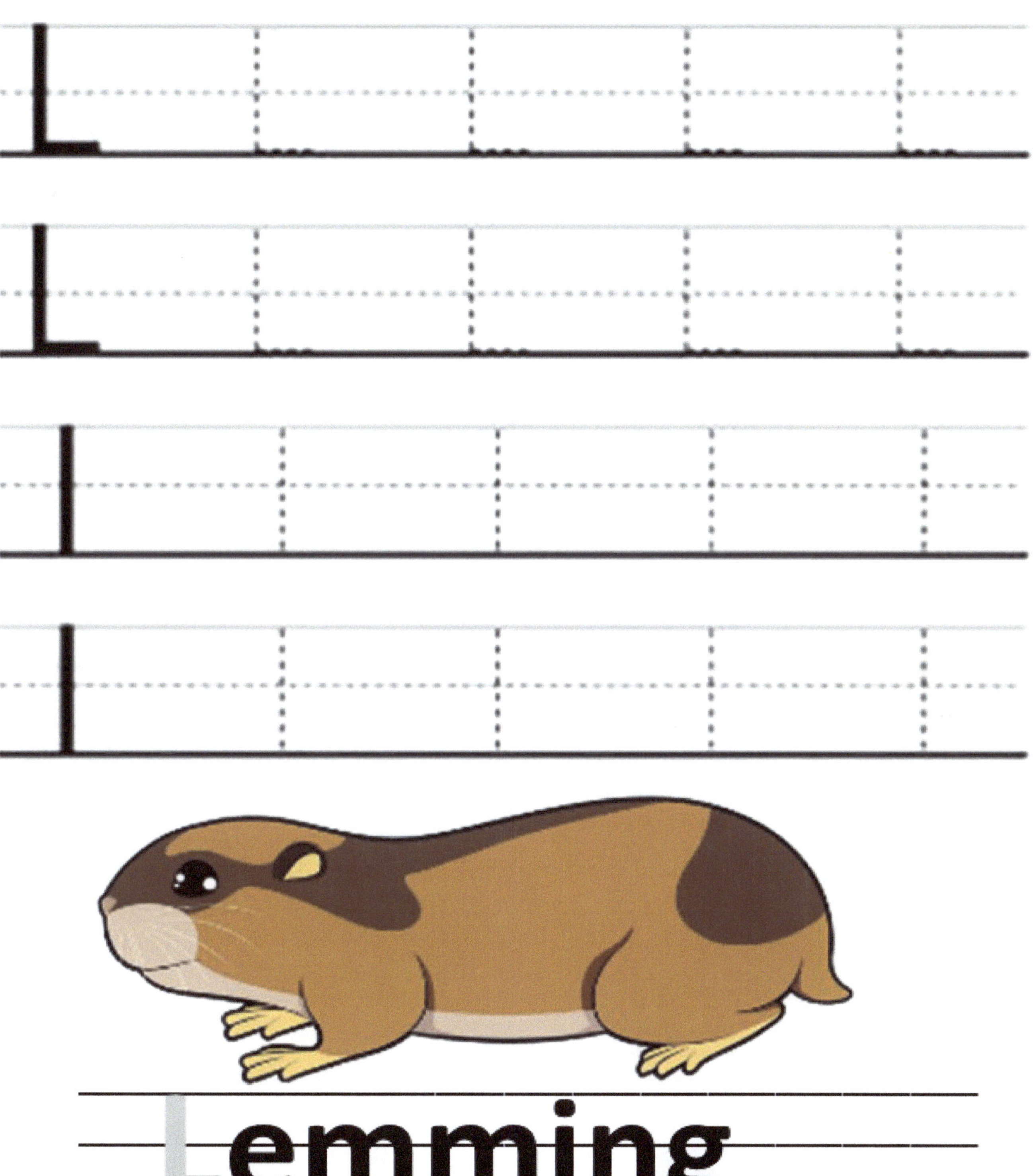

Lemming

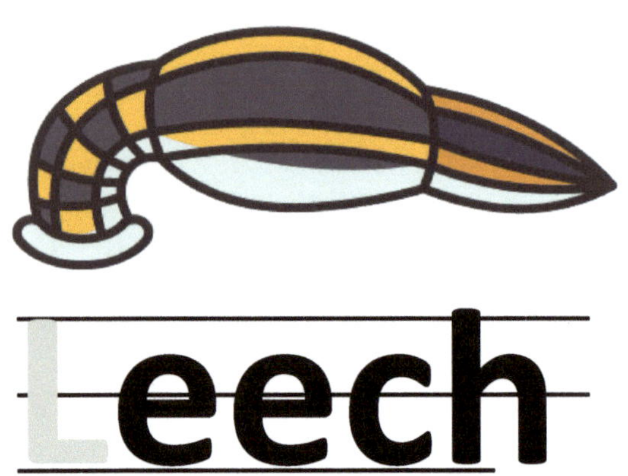

Leech

Leopard

Lion

Lizard

Lobster

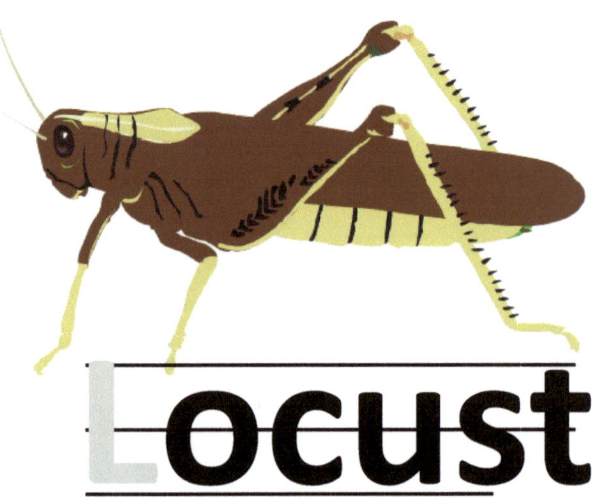

Locust

Mm

Moos

Mamba

Macaw

Moth

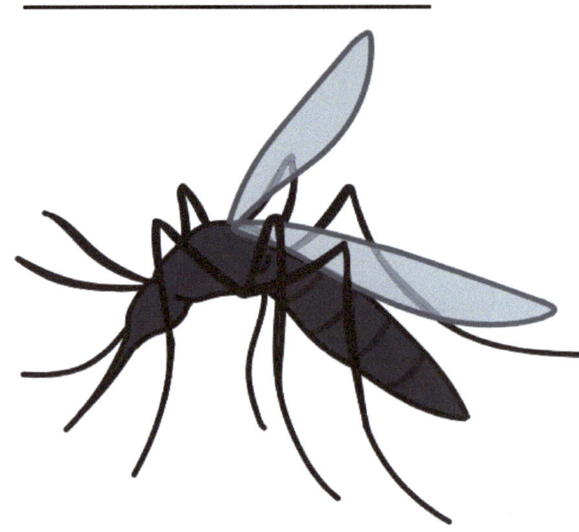

Mosquito

Mule

Mole

Nn

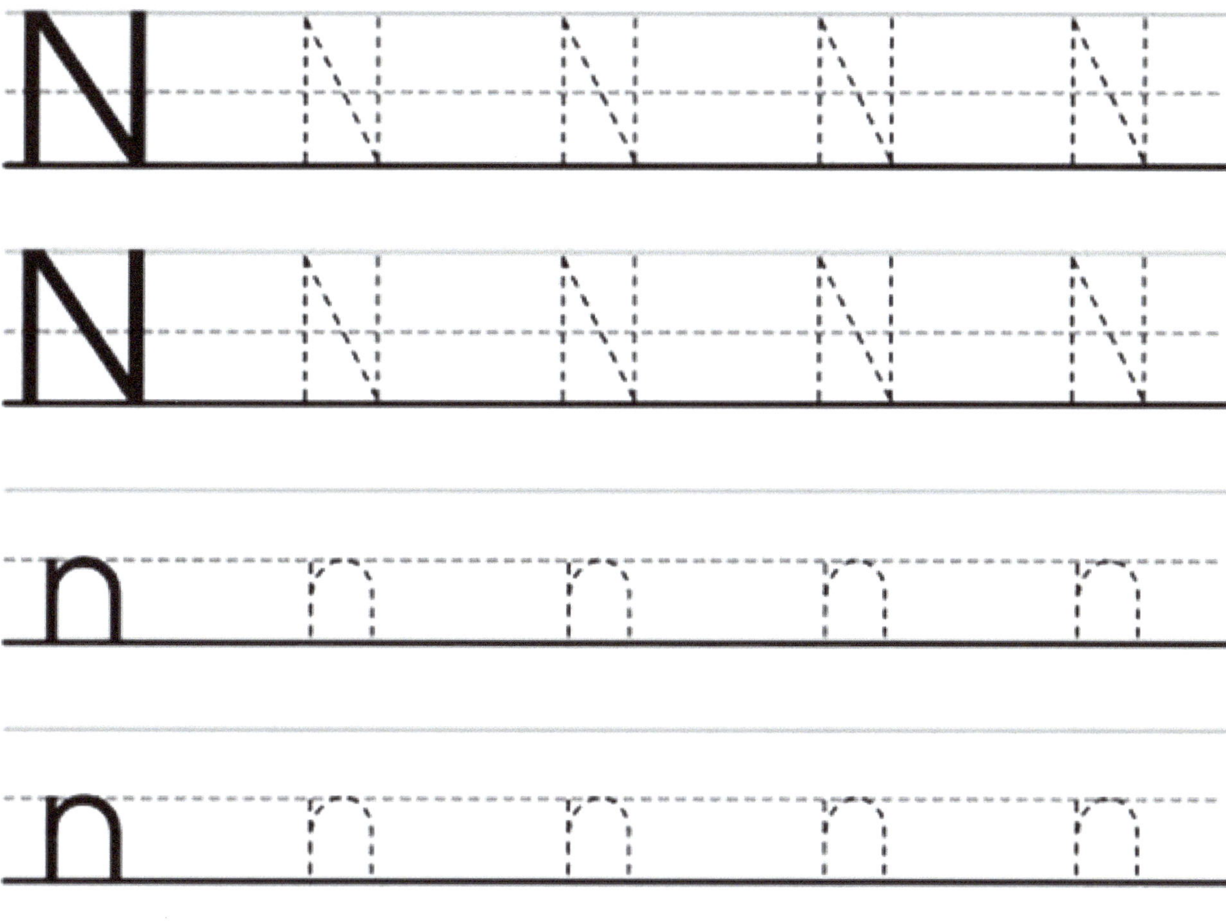

Night Heron

Newt

Nyala

Nilgai

Numbat

Nightingale

Neon Tetra

Oo

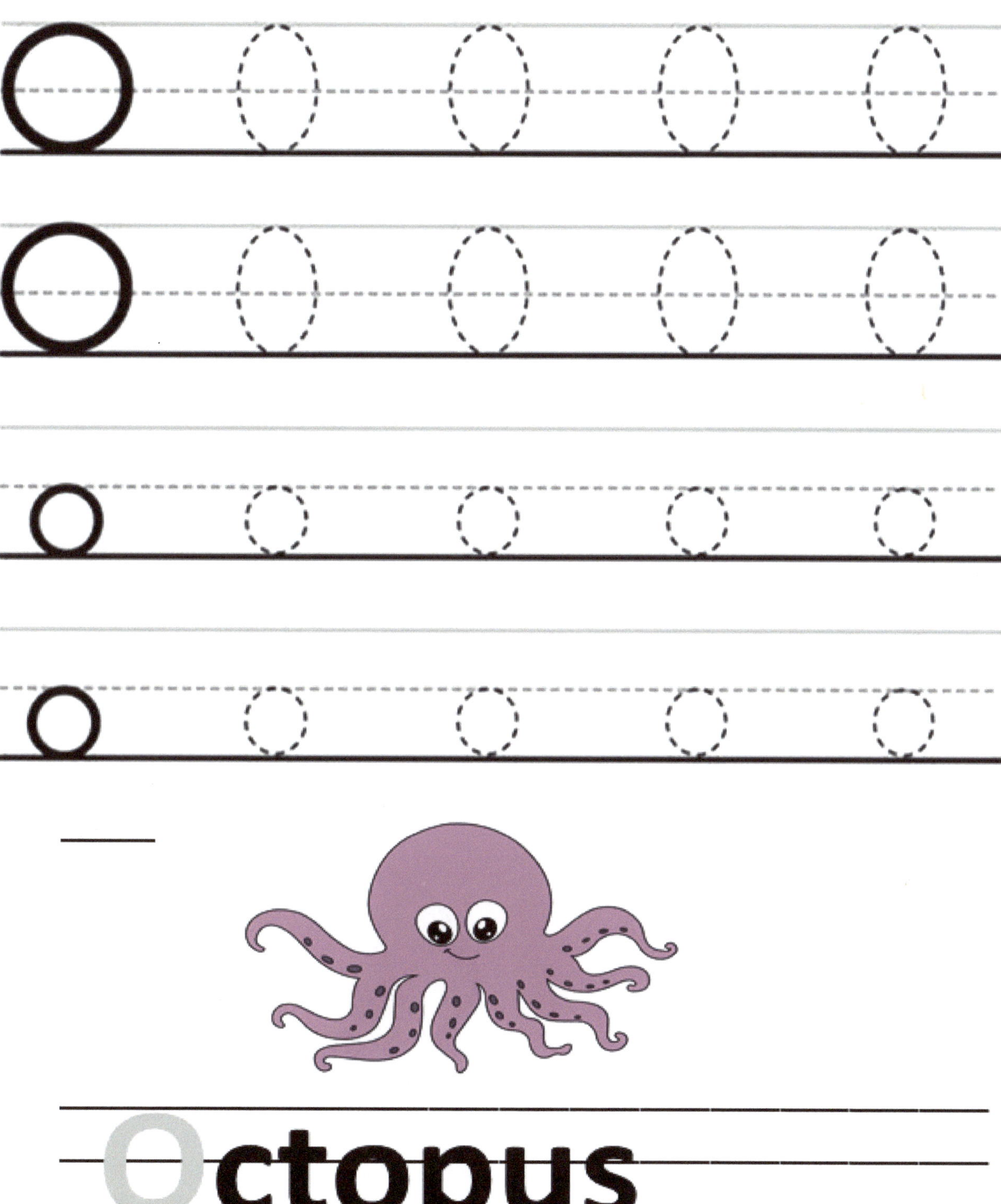

Octopus

Otter

Owl

Ostrich

Ox

Olm

Oyster

Pp

P P P P P

P P P P P

p p p p p

p p p p p

Panther

Peacock

Pelican

Parrot

Pig

Python

Qq

Q

Q

q

q

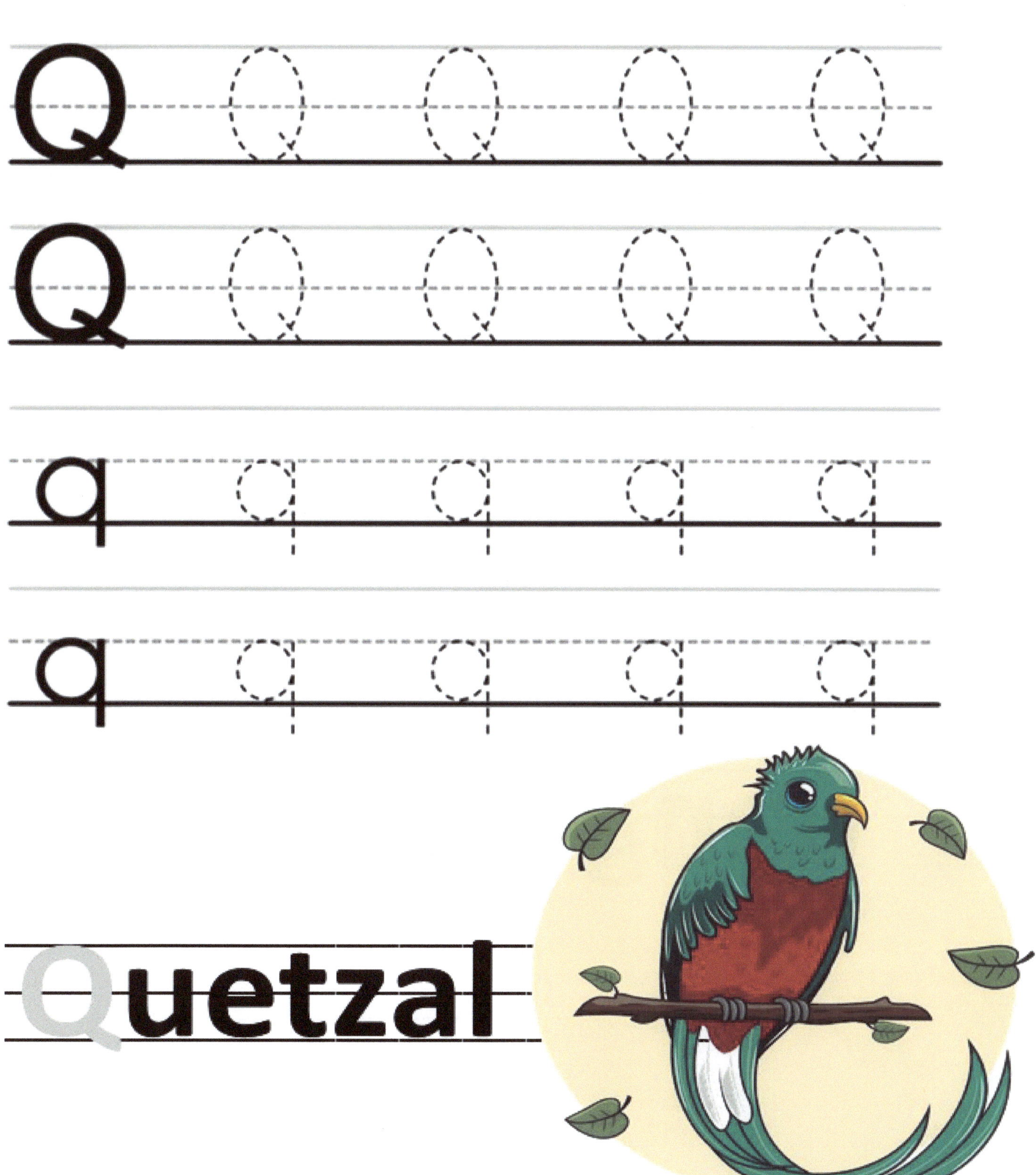

Quetzal

Queen Snake

Quail

Quanga

Quoll

Quokka

Rr

R R R R R

R R R R R

r r r r r

r r r r r

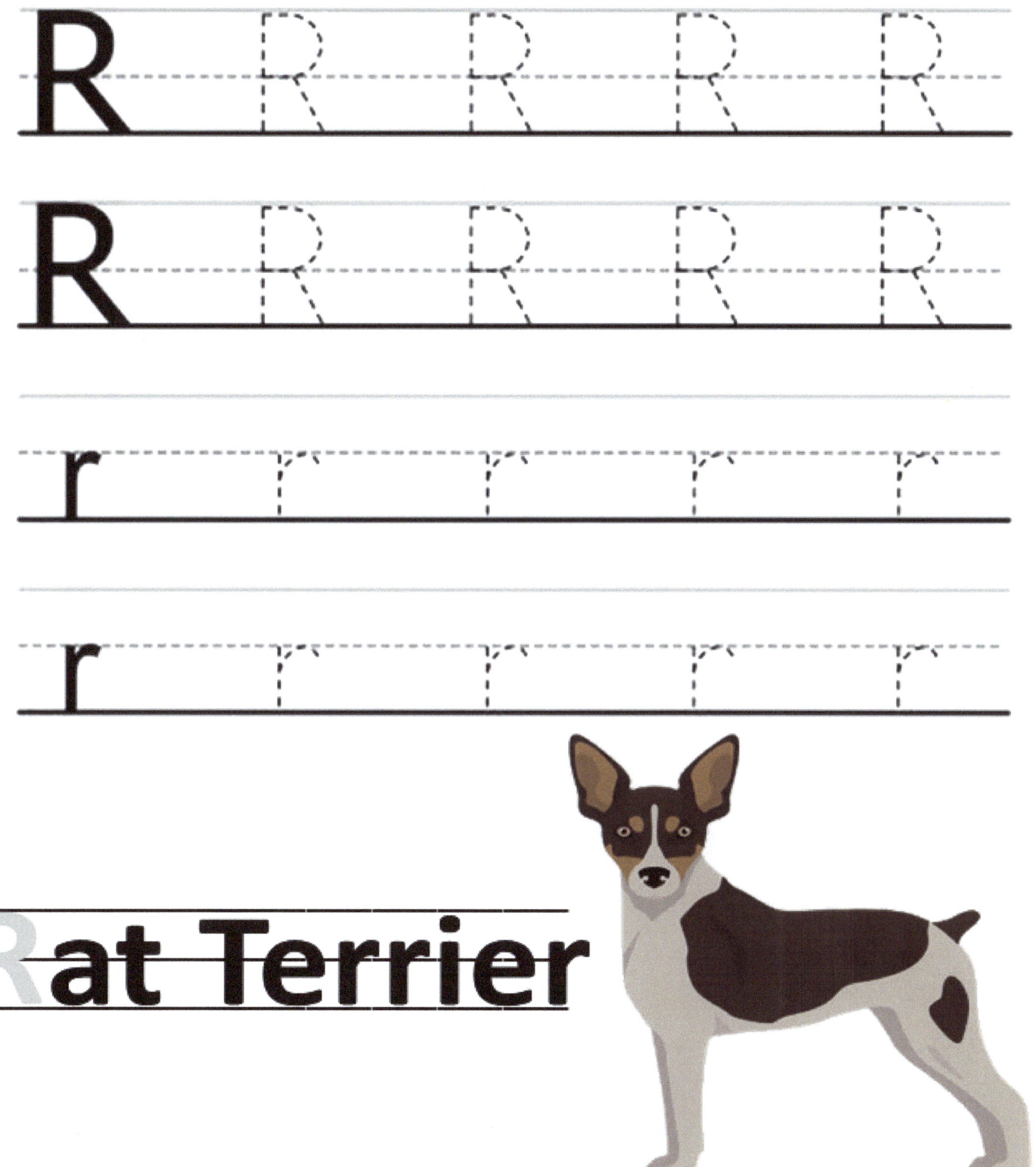

Rat Terrier

Rabbit

Racoon

Rat

Robin

Reindeer

Rhino

Ss

S   S   S   S   S

S   S   S   S   S

s   s   s   s   s

s   s   s   s   s

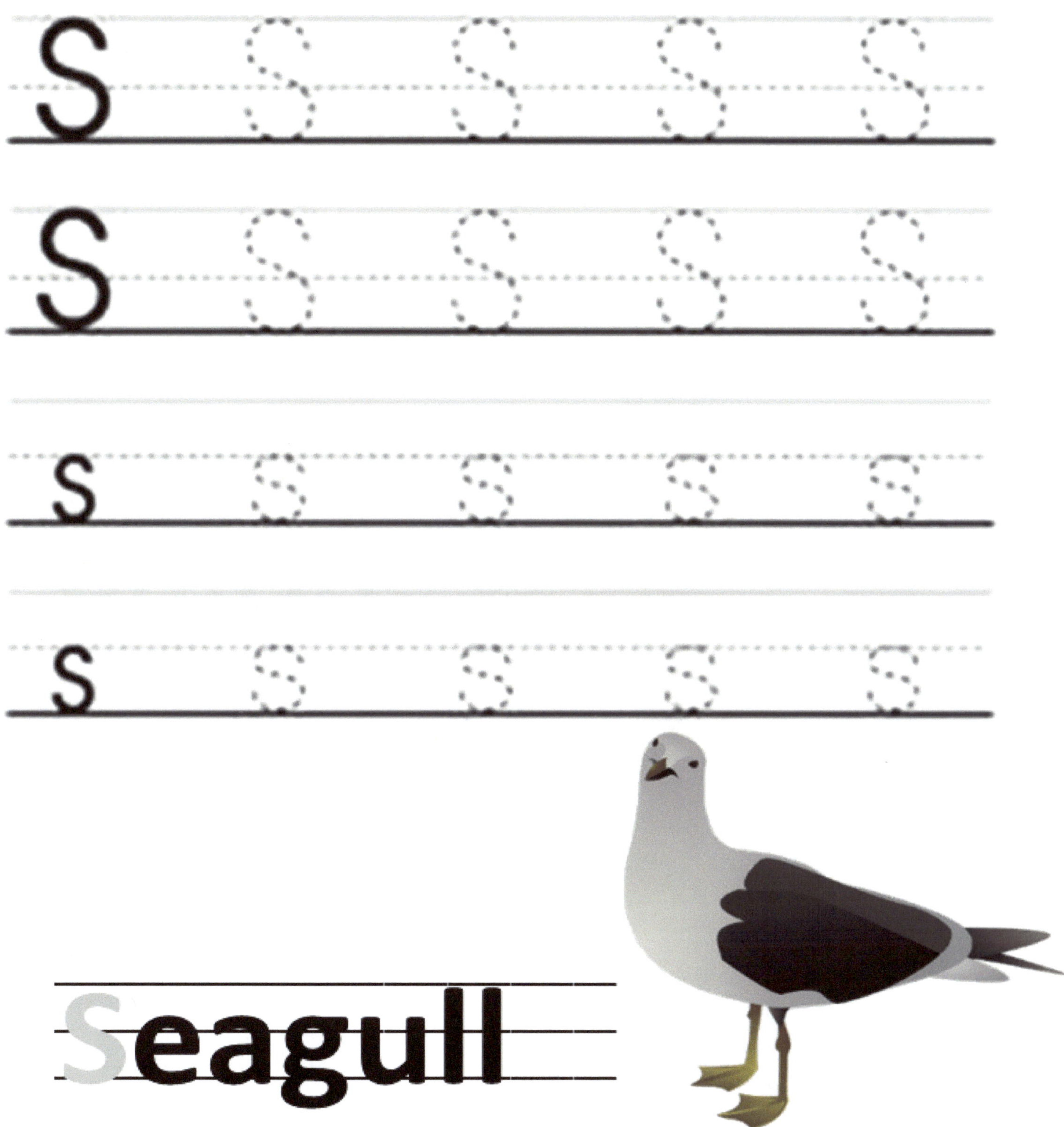

Seagull

Snake

Snail

Sparrow

Shrimp

Squirrel

Stork

Learn to write

Tt

T T T T T

T T T T T

t t t t t

t t t t t

Taco

Terrier

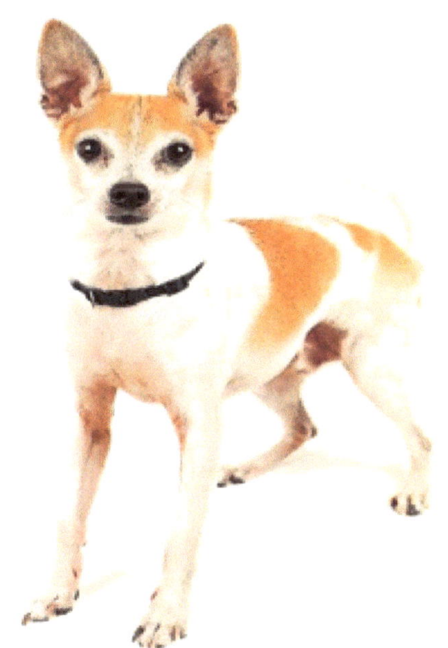

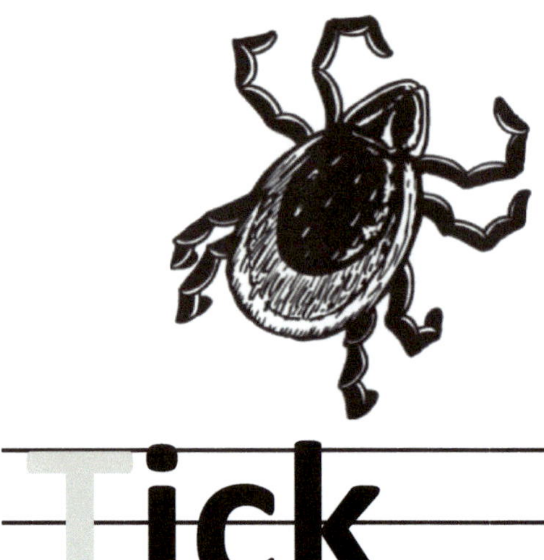

Tick

Tiger

Tuna

Turkey

Turtle

Tarsier

Uu

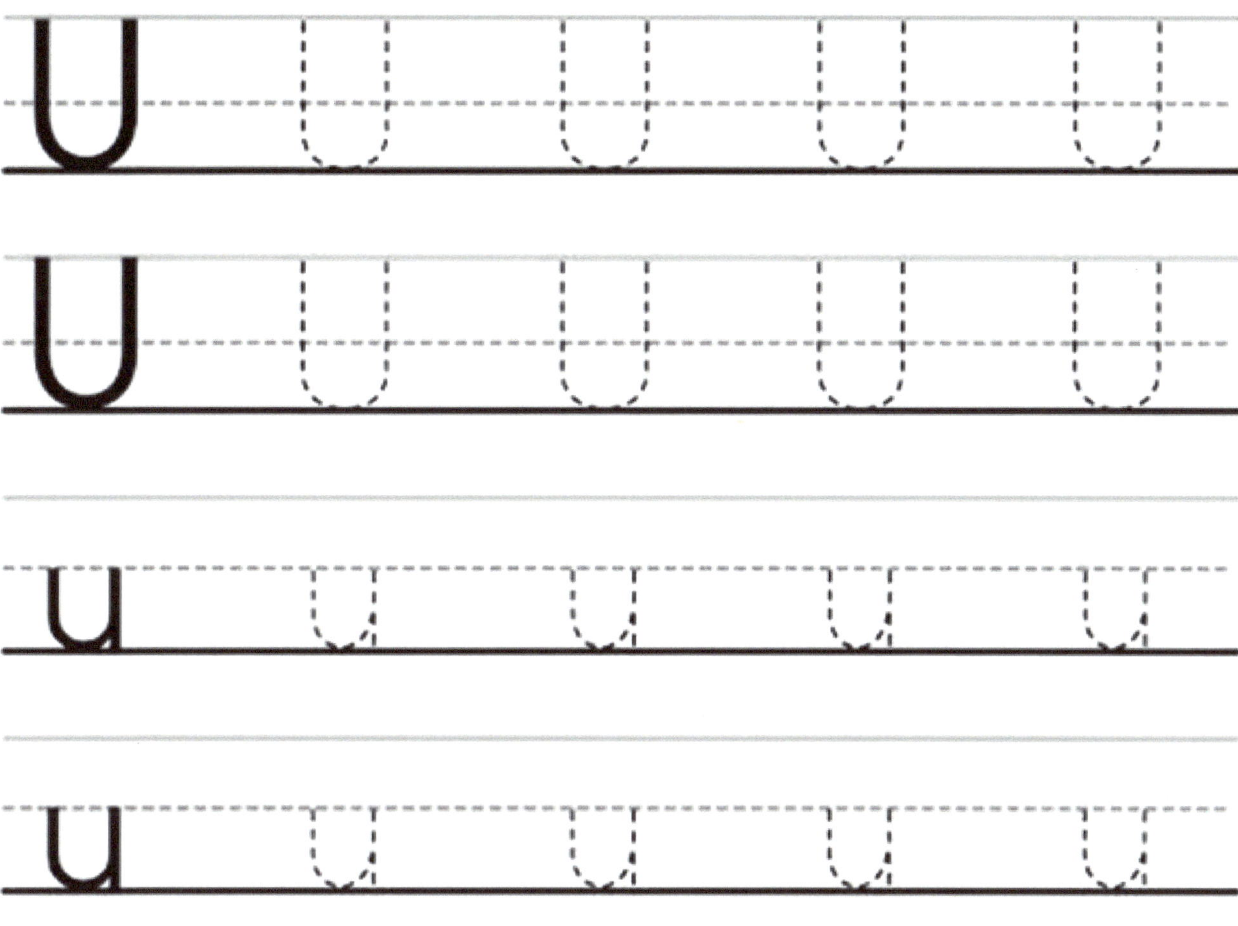

Uakari

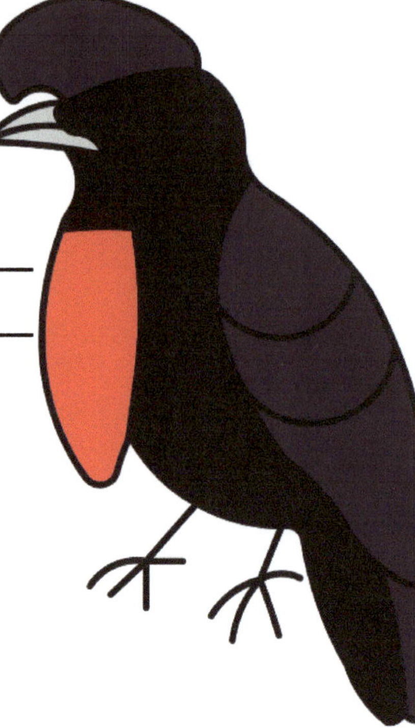

Umbrellabird

Unau

Uguisu

Vv

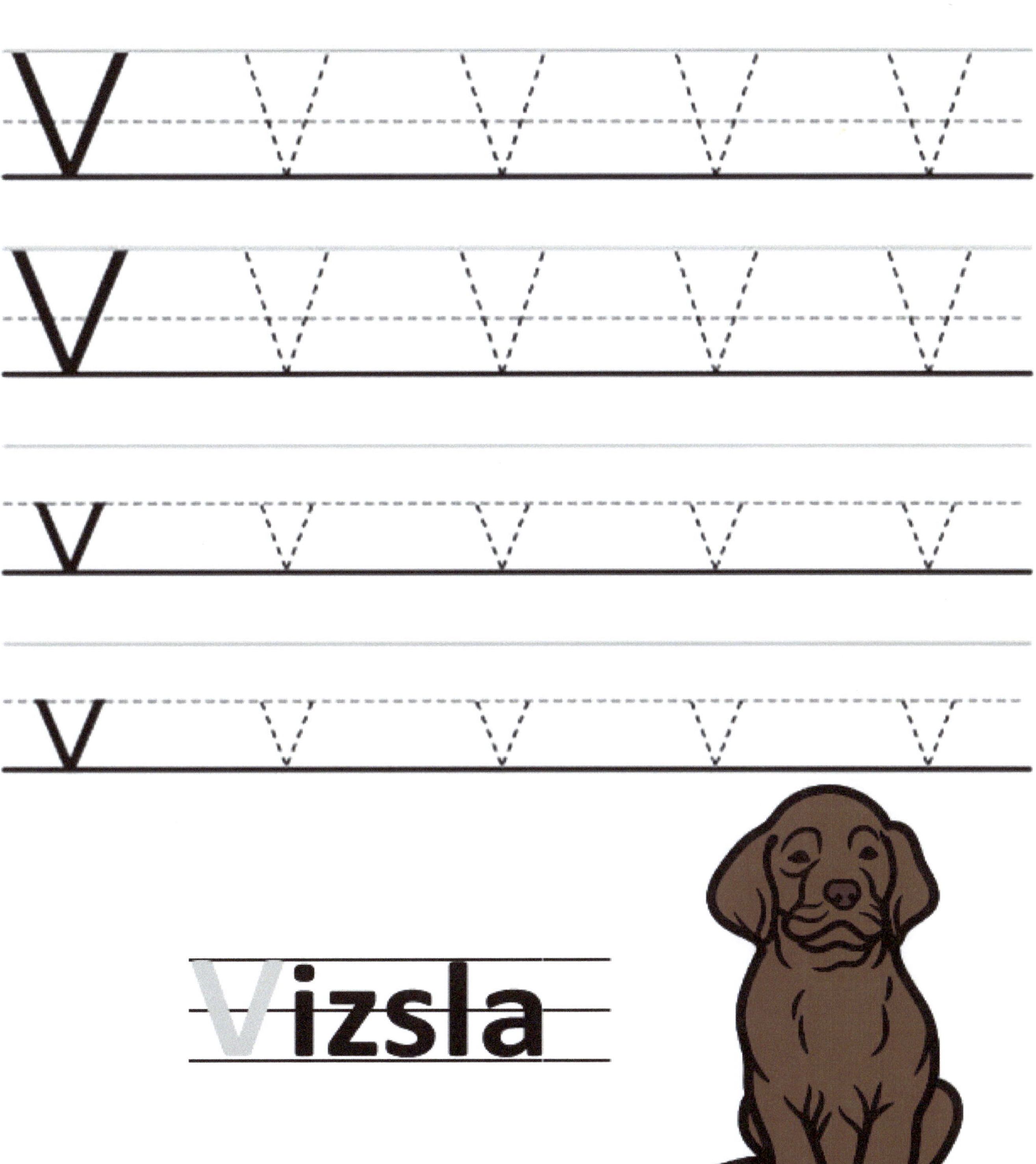

Vulture

Viper

Vicuña

Vaquita

Ww

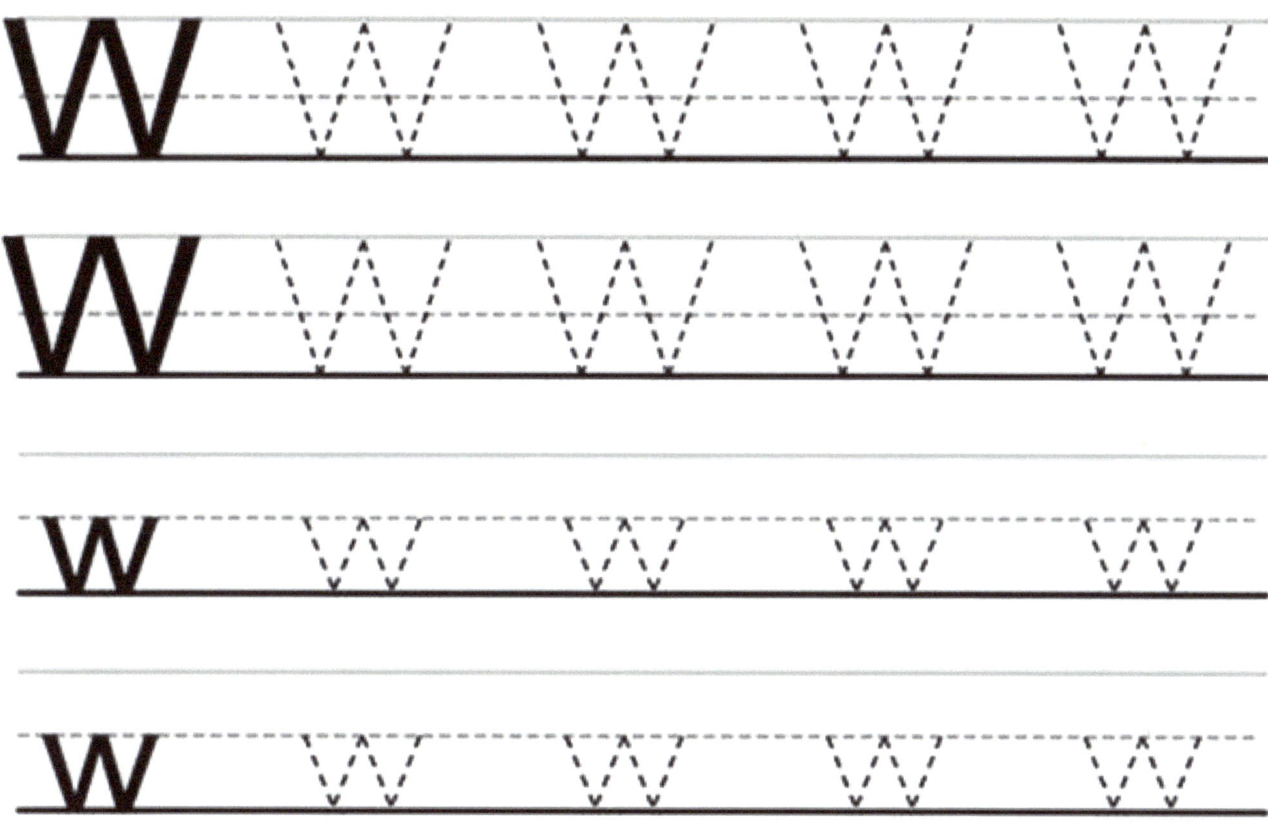

Wolf

Wasp

Weasel

Walrus

Warthog

Whippet

Wallaby

Rr

R R R R R

R R R R R

r r r r r

r r r r r

Rat Terrier

Xerus

Xeme

X-ray Tetra

Yy

Yarara

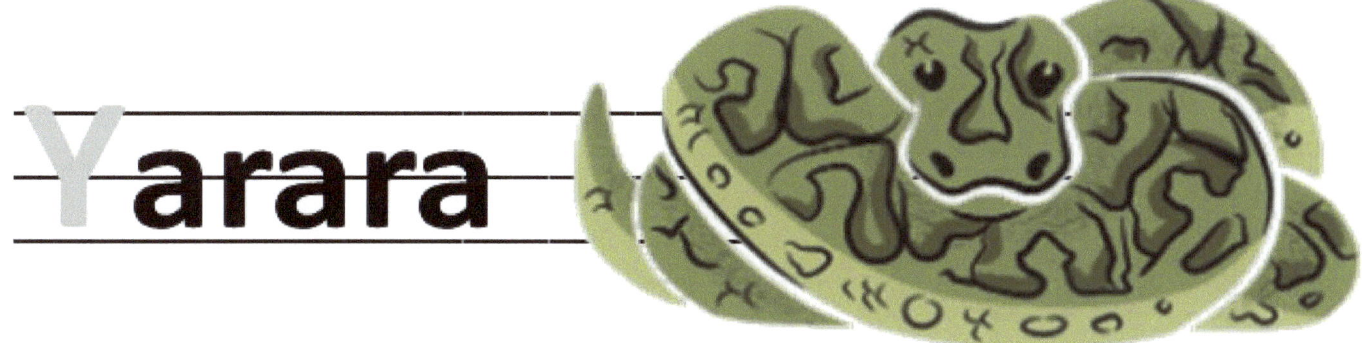

Yak

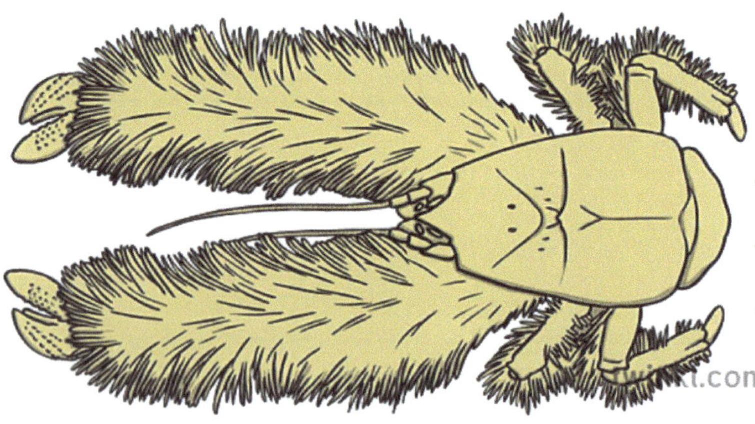

Yeti Crab

Yellow
Perch

Zz

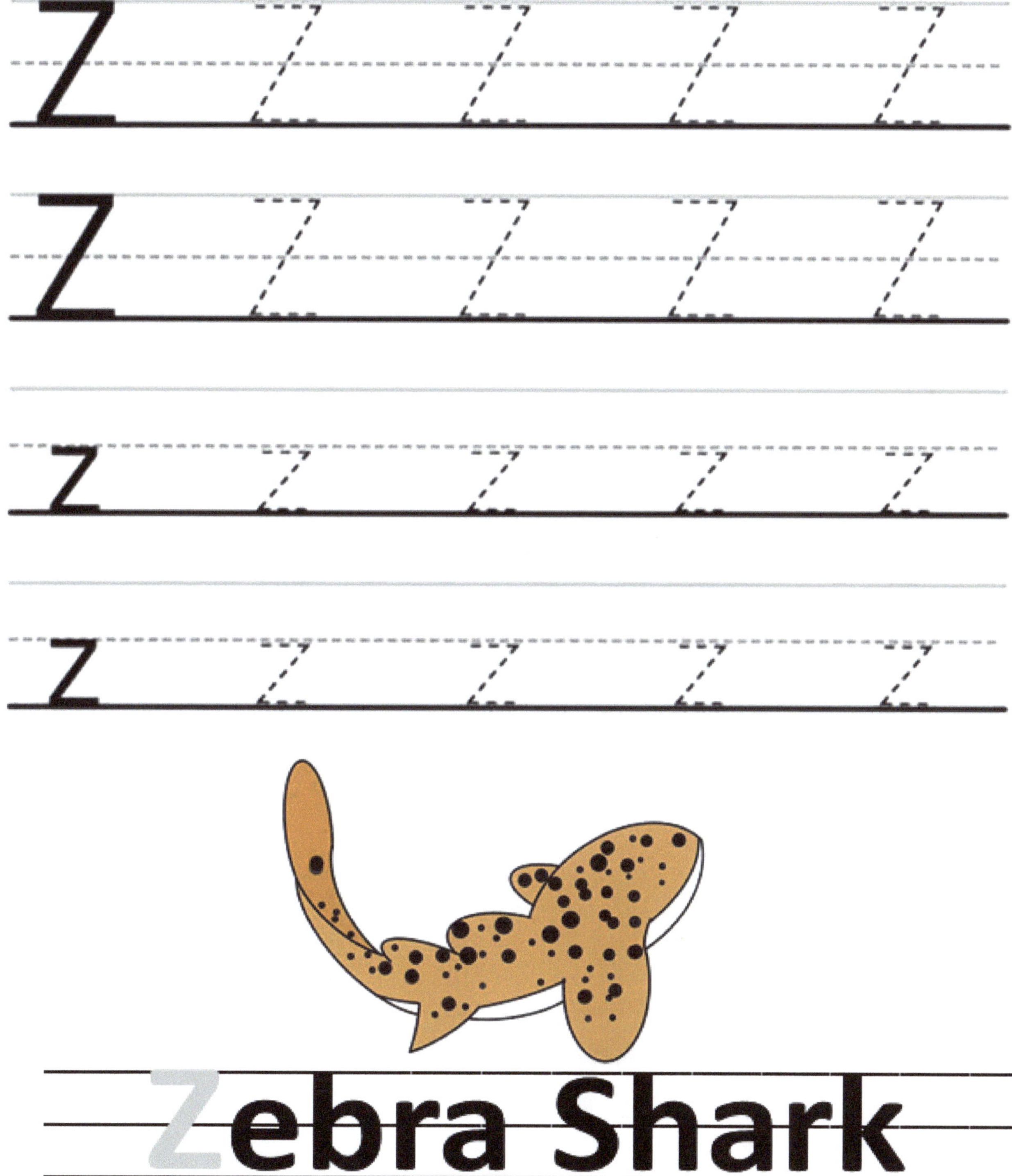

Zebra

Zonkey

Zebu

Zuchon

ISBN
Hardbound- 978-621-470-351-7
Softbound/Paperback-978-621-470-352-4
MOBI/KINDLE-978-621-470-353-1

Published by:
Poetry Planet Book Publishing House
Rosario, Pozorrubio, Pangasinan, Philippines
Contact No.: 09554960044
Email: maritesritumalta@gmail.com

ROY B. BASA
LPT, PhD, DHum, DMin, DSc, FPOd, FRIEdr

Roy Basa was born and raised in Murcia, Negros Occidental, Philippines by Raul and Lilia Basa together with his other 6 siblings. He graduated his elementary education from Lopez Jaena Elementary School.

He then went to La Consolacion College, Murcia for his secondary education where he graduated as Class Valedictorian. He got his Bachelor's in Education major in General Science, Master's in School Administration and Supervision, and Doctor of Philosophy major in Educational Management at the University of Negros Occidental – Recoletos where he graduated with Outstanding Dissertation and High Academic Distinction Awards. He then took another masterate, the Master in Natural Science at the University of St. La Salle, Bacolod under a scholarship grant, Project – Free Paglaum.

He was a high school, college, and graduate school science teacher for 18 years in the Philippines and 3 years as a high school science teacher in Arizona and New Mexico, USA, respectively.

He was awarded as one of the Most Outstanding Teachers of the Philippines in 2016 by the Metrobank Foundation, Philippines. Recently, he was also awarded by Asia – Pacific Luminare Awards as "Asia's Most Remarkable and Exceptional Science and CTE Educator of the Year 2022.

ROZEL JAENA BASA, MBA

Rozel Jaena Basa was born in Bacolod City and raised in Murcia, Negros Occidental, Philippines by Romeo and Razel Jaena together with her other 3 siblings. She graduated with her elementary education from Murcia Elementary School. She then went to La Consolacion College, Murcia for her secondary education. She got her Bachelor of Science in Information Management and Master's in Business Administration at the University of Negros Occidental – Recoletos

She was a former Manager at Golden Sun Finance Corporation, Bacolod City, Philippines for 16 years. Recently, she is one of the Educational Assistants for Pre – K to 2 at Shiwi Ts'ana Elementary School, Zuni, New Mexico, USA.